Not yours, Truly

Giselle Chan

For my sister, who pays for McDonald's every time I "forget" my wallet.

TABLE OF CONTENTS

ACKNOWLEDGMENTS

Infinite gratitude for:

My family, who will buy this book and never read it, but continues to support me tirelessly.

Ben, Ana, and Nicole, without whom this book would have never been published.

Mr. MacLean, Ms. Hoover, and Ms. Izadpanah, who nurtured my love for writing.

Brian, who teaches and inspires me to become a better artist in every way.

Kristy, Megan, and Isaac, who have read most of this book before I even decided to publish it.

Everyone who read my handwritten novels in elementary school and unknowingly encouraged me to publish this.

God, who taught me how to love because He first loved us.

GUTS

Guts. Guts.

"Guys, please keep moving."

Guts. That's the only thing you can think of—guts. Guts, guts, and more guts. Back in grade two, you thought guts was a curse word. You tested it in the back of your dentals until it reached the tip of your tongue in quiet, rebellious whispers to yourself in class, on the bus, and at home. By the time grade three rolled around, you freely said the word out loud all the time upon realizing it was not a curse word at all.

"Guts," you would scream across the playground at the skinny eight year old boy who yanked at your hair all the time, "I hate your guts sooo much!" All through October and November, screaming would ensue all across the playground as all the other third graders began running around, echoing your words in shrill voices amidst the damp fall weather and mushy leaves. *You* were the one who started the trend of incorporating "guts" into your colloquial vocabulary.

"Guys, *guys*."

The last time you said the word "guts" was probably grade three. The word's popularity had fizzled out by grade four and it was no longer so satisfying on your tongue. The last time you even thought about the word "guts" was probably over a decade ago. In your mind, it was categorized as a childish and immature word. A word reserved for the colourful plastic playground. But right now, it was the word stuck in your head, ringing in circles louder than the third graders from the playground.

"Don't look down, please, just keep moving!"

"Guys! Move, please!"

Come to think of it, "guys" was just a one letter difference away from "guts".

You allow yourself to glance down.

"Keep moving!"

You suck in, swallow, and regret it instantly.

You become aware of the unsettling silence in between the gaps of shuffling feet around you. It's heavy and unsure of where to go and it oozes off of every surface—your skin, the metal, your bag, the man's briefcase next to you. It's not like it's totally silent. The silence is more of a presence, the manifestation of an undeniable, irreversible truth that everyone wishes they hadn't witnessed today. The smell of smoke hangs heavily in the air. Your feet follow the other sets of shuffling feet, unsure of where to go. They feel like lead. You were supposed to be going to meet Leslie for lunch.

"Priority One," announces the intercom loudly, "Priority One on Line One heading southbound. This train is now out of service."

Everyone files out on to the platform, still cloaked in the dead silence. You realize that some women are screaming despite the silence—high shrieks, but those were deadened by the heaviness that clung to everybody's ears. The silence screamed louder than they did.

Your feet take you to the escalator that leads you up, up and away. You usually take the stairs and you're sure some of the other witnesses do too, but no one bothers to walk them. Your eyes are so dry that they hurt—maybe it's from the smoke. When you blink, you can hear the small sound of your contacts sticking and unsticking against your eyelids. Your ears can hear the sounds that are so normal around you. The beep when you exit the station gates sounds normal. The sliding of the automatic doors sounds normal. The sound of passing cars when you exit the station and on to the street sounds normal. The sound of the wind brushing past your ears sounds normal. Your chest hurts.

I'll have to cancel on lunch today. Not feeling so well. Will take a rain check on this one. So sorry!

Silence is thick and clings at your clothes. You have to force yourself to begin walking. You don't know where, but you want to go. You want to go anywhere but here. You don't know where you're going at all.

"Wake up," you croak pleadingly to yourself under your breath, "wake up, dammit." You're not even sure if any sound came out at all.

Guts. There is no escape from the word.

There is a park to the right. Some kids are playing a rough game of tag in the grass. One of the girls, the smallest one, is tagged by a taller boy. She stomps her feet angrily before setting off, chasing another boy, screeching: "I hate your guts! You're gonna be *sooo* sorry!"

The boy retaliates with some sort of taunt, but you can't make out what he says at all. You gag. You try to swallow it down and gag again. You can't hold it back and grey puke splatters all over the grass next to the sidewalk. It's lumpy and chunky.

"Fuck," you whisper.

Panting, you put your hands on your knees for a while before straightening up. All you see is a green and grey blur. Was that some red? Your watery eyes make everything blur together. Guts, guts, guts, insists your brain.

Wake up, wake up, wake up, you say back desperately. Someone won't be waking up tomorrow, you realize in your gut.

You force yourself to take the deepest breath of fresh and damp October air that you can muster. It doesn't smell fresh at all. It smells like metal, burning flesh, and guts. You can even taste it.

A ROOM IN MY HOUSE, BUT IT'S NOT MINE

I used to talk a lot, you know. That's what everyone around me tells me. I used to be fun to hang out with, fun to talk to, and a bit too over the top. They tell me that I've been becoming a different person lately. They tell me that I've changed a lot since they've first met me. I think it's because I talk less. Do you think that's the reason why? I'm not sure.

There's a crushing amount of stuff in my head. Maybe you know already from the dark grey lines underneath my eyes. But I've also put on layers and layers of beige goop until my skin sags and droops under its weight, so you might not be able to see those lines. To me though, they're still plain and exposed under any lighting. The goop doesn't seem to help hide them very much, despite other people constantly reassuring me that they don't see anything.

Anyway, like I said, I haven't been feeling like myself lately. By "lately," I actually mean for what's felt like a long time because I don't remember how long it's been, either… all I know is that it feels like it's been forever since I've started feeling this way. Does that make sense?

Honestly, I've lost track of time so badly that I don't even remember how long I've been talking to you.

When did we even start meeting regularly? Have you been sitting there the whole time?

I know you're supposed to help, but I don't know, what are you doing exactly? I'm still drowning. It hurts to breathe. You just nod often, and once in a while, you'll give me a weird look. Your head is going to fall off from all the nodding. I'm not blaming you; I guess I don't know if I expected something different. By now, I'm in so much pain I just feel sort of numb, really. I don't know what I'm saying. How can someone hurt and feel numb at the same time? Everything about myself is a mess. I'm confused. I just want to give up.

...Give up?...

Well, let's just get on with this. I guess I'll start with the man. When I walk home from work and the skies are already dark, there is a man. He is a little older than me, I think, by a few years at least. Every time I walk past the intersection at Heatherwood and Second Street, he is standing under the bus shelter on the other side of the road, watching me with a wide smile. Ever since I was a kid, I really enjoyed the early sunset in the Winter months, but I haven't been able to enjoy it the same ever since I noticed him. His outline is clear in the darkness and his body takes on a luminescent shape against the contrasting backdrop. Something about him makes my intestines twist because he looks so familiar, but I can never quite put my finger on it. He's always smiling. Ever since I saw him for the first time, I've been feeling sick to my stomach. My mouth goes dry.

...So tired… tiring...

I always see him at that intersection. But he expands—he expands beyond the intersection. I've been seeing him more and more often as time progresses. He has expanded to meet me at work when I stay overtime and even in the confines of my home. Once, I even saw him in the middle of the night when I was half-asleep and going to the washroom. He freaked me so much that night that I ran back to my room and hid under my duvet until light filled the room and I was sure he was no longer there.

There's something else to him—he sends me these whisperers throughout the day and the night. To explain: they're these relentless things that do exactly what you think—they whisper. I mean, for the most part. Some of them like to sing things into my ears. Some of the other ones yell or shriek. I cannot make out most of the words even though they're so loud. The stuff that they say sounds like nonsense, usually. Of what I can make out, I catch some snippets of English, but it sounds almost like a different language. The things that I do understand are usually mean. At other times, they just whisper completely random things. Twice, they've sung the news forecast opening music to me. What are they telling me? Why are they doing this? Am I going to die? Can I?

I should have brought this up earlier! That's what you're going to tell me. How long has this been going on?

I don't know!

But what's the point? There doesn't seem to be an escape from this; I know that you won't be able to help me anyway.

As time goes on, the whisperers multiply and they hiss into my ears fouler things. This makes me feel less inclined to tell you about the man. Whenever I do feel even the slightest urge to tell you, he silences me with a smile.

...Don't forget to smile!...

That smile is a powerful one. Although it appears to be friendly, it freezes me from my core. It starts at my tailbone, goes up into my torso, down my limbs, up to wrap around my neck, and leaves my eyes feeling raw.

Repeat the words? The whisperers' words? I can't—there are too many. They vomit words, sounds, and songs at me so fast that I can't help but drown all of it. Even when I'm at work—they're merciless. My boss isn't happy with me.

Smile!

He's standing behind you right now, actually.

...Hello...

Yes. What? Of course he's smiling. He's here, and he's smiling. He smiles like he knows something about me that I don't; it's just terrifying. I don't know what to do anymore! Why won't stop smiling?

...We're all in your head...

What? Why are you telling me that these voices aren't real? They are! I know they are. Why would I lie to you? They probably want you to believe that they're not real—that I'm just psycho. I'm a lunatic. This is why I haven't told anyone. You, of all people, I thought might understand.

Listen, I can prove that they're real. Their words make me sick. I'm always cold—can't you tell from my heavy turtlenecks? Yes, of course I know it's summertime. I'm so cold I can barely move my fingers right now. I'm nauseous. I have headaches. They burrow at my insides and hollow me out, so that I will eventually shatter. They're just waiting until I finally do. I wonder if they will continue to torture me even after I've shattered.

Unlike the man, the whisperers aren't visible, but they're definitely there. I can feel them on my skin, touching me and sucking on to me like leeches. I can't shake them off. I shower at least three times a day. Exfoliating and scrubbing doesn't work. My skin looks yellow and holds a strange sensation of raw and sticky. I can't sleep and my chest is always so tight and constricted. I try to take my inhaler before I go to bed, too. It doesn't help. What do I do?

The whisperers loom over me in the same way angry storm clouds and heavy waves hound an already sinking ship. Its masts are in flames. I'm freezing and on fire at the same time. I'm trapped in a room. I'm screaming. My voice doesn't go anywhere. There's no door in this room. I can't even hear my own voice because it's drowned out by the whisperers. I just want to be left alone.

...We're here for you...

The man knows something about me. Why does he remind me of something from the past? He reminds me of a musky, purple scent and the odor of perspiration. He brings memories of panic back to me. Maybe I once found this scent attractive—maybe erotic, even. Terror rises in my chest—it's too tight! I can't breathe, but somehow I'm screaming.

I've tried so hard to forget this. I almost want to find that purple scent attractive again. The man breathes down my neck. The scent makes me gag. In my sleep, I've tried begging him to stop. It's only in my dreams that I'm able to speak to him. He just ignores me. He shakes his head "no". I want to kill myself for letting myself to be touched by this man.

Have I tried ignoring him? Are you serious? How do I ignore something that is constantly hovering around me? Listen, the whisperers point out what I've done wrong in everything I say or do. Believe me, I've tried to drown them out, but it's impossible. There are so many of them that their voices are inescapable. I brought this upon myself, they keep saying.

...It was on you though...

I know, I know this already! God, you don't have to tell me again.

But they don't stop. Why won't they stop? They know me. They whisper things that happened years ago that I thought no one would ever know about. How do they know about that? Why do they know everything about me?

What did they whisper to me? Wait! Just listen:

...Yeah, but you let him, though...

Oh yeah, and then they laugh.

They laugh! It's not even funny!

He always said things that made me feel good; how could I not let him say them to me? Of course I believed them. He made me feel good about myself. How come he makes me feel so scared now? What happened? I listened and clung to everything he said. I thought he was beautiful. God, I'd probably still believe whatever he said to me. He told me he didn't like to hear me cry.

...Should have cried louder then!...

I know, I know, I cried. I couldn't help it. I didn't mean to. He told me, at least, if I can't stop crying, that I shouldn't make any noise, so I didn't say anything for the rest of that day. I mean, I get it. That's what I was always told in school. I keep quiet; I stay in single file lines. I always got good grades, didn't I? I'm good at following instructions. I followed all his instructions. Where did I go wrong? Purple musk envelops my neck and fills up my nostrils.

My parents always said to obey my elders. It would be disrespectful if I refused his orders. I let him whisper these things into my body nine years ago, and the most disappointing thing about myself is that I would be the same if I saw him again. I can't refuse him. I don't think I'll ever become strong enough to.

You let him,

You let him,

They chant all the time in shrieking whispers—but I never knew I said yes. I never knew I said yes to the man who I saw smiling under the bus shelter. He smiles the same way as he did nine years ago on the living room sofa, while the news on the TV blared on and on.

Hey, don't forget to smile!...

There are only two people in this room, though.

...See you...

"See you next week," she says.

PORCELAIN

On the corner of the Main Street corridor, there was a dimly lit cafe decorated with wooden planks and multiple paintings of nothing in particular hung on the brown walls. The permanent smell of coffee clung to the small unit, and the longer you stayed in the cafe, the stronger the aroma clung to your jacket when you left. In the sweltering heat of the summer, visitors came to order their icy caffeinated drinks and the little room was filled with chatter and clinking ice cubes in glasses. But right now, in the ashen greyness of Winter, the greyness seemed to linger everywhere, even on the warm brown walls inside. The servers lit candles—but they only helped a little bit. Amidst the grey, a young girl with a brown coat walked into the cafe, her glasses lens fogging up. Upon her arrival, the boy looked up from the counter and gestured to one of the small round tables at the back.

The girl took off her brown coat and hung it on the chair. Some snow from her hair fell to the floor as she sat down. A little glazed over, her eyes swept over the dim little room, taking in the flickering candle lit windows, brown walls, and faded art frames. The boy hurriedly brought over a tea bag steeped in steaming water in a tiny, white porcelain cup. Nodding her silent thanks, she took a sip, eyes still glazed over as she stared at nothing in particular. The boy lingered near her table; he had something to say.

She stayed still, only moving to sip at her steaming tea. She looked like a doll when her eyes glazed over like that, with pale white skin and dark lashes that framed her face. She looked small, pale, and fragile, just like the porcelain cup she was holding. The boy hesitated, then said, "How have you been doing lately?"

She acknowledged his question with a small nod accompanied with a mumble saying she was okay, and her eyes drifted over to him and held his for a while. A moment later, her eyes then broke their gaze and slid down to study the cup that she held. There was a crack on the handle, which connected to the rest of the cup. The crack stretched across the bottom of the handle and wove its way up the material, but it did not reach the body of the cup. She sipped some of the tea.

"Dried raspberry and I also added some nettle leaf," he said, explaining the tea.

The boy looked nervous; he wanted to leave, but he continued to linger by her like there was an unseen, but tangible connection hidden within her slight body and behind her porcelain exterior pulling him close. He went to the other side of the table and sat in the chair across from her.

"You like it, right? I added some extra leaves into the bag too.

This tea should be good for you. Given, you know, that, you know, you're..."

She cut him off with a mumbled okay, thanks. Silence ensued between the two young people and they sat like that for a long time. The candlelight cast their long silhouettes against the brown walls. While they bathed in silence, the world outside bathed in ash. The number of cars and people dwindled under the sky closing in with the inevitable night. The boy stood up, taking her cup, and took it to the kitchen.

He came back quickly, holding the white cup by the handle, and being careful not to spill freshly boiled hot water. He took a seat across from her.

She nodded her thanks again in silence, taking the cup with both hands and sipping hot tea. The tea bag was still very strong.

By now, the snow on her jacket had melted and even the puddle beneath her feet had dried up in the warmth of the coffee fragrant room. They sat like that, with the boy's eyes on her and with her eyes focused on nothing in particular, just glazed over. He took her in wholly—from her slender shoulders to her small hands curled around the cup, the silver pendant that always hung at her collarbones to her curved waist which he had once been so familiar with. She was so familiar that he could still remember the small mole on her right hip and the small heart tattooed on the side of her rib cage.

"You're just the same as you were before."

It was a lie, she looked the same, but without a doubt, he felt that she was very different since he last talked with her in the angry phone call. She heard his comment, but she did not say anything in response. It seemed like a one-sided battle. She listened carefully to what he had to say, but her eyes were focused on the cup with its cracked handle. He did not let her silence deter him. He spoke again, "You still look the same. You're still very beautiful."

Perhaps he thought this would warm her up enough to talk, but it did not. She would not look up and she was not warm.

Dejected, he fell back into silence again, but he felt like he should say something. It would be the right thing to do. He stared down at the table, awkward, and his hands fidgeted with one another. He wished he had something to hold in his hands. His palms were sticky with sweat. The shop would be closing soon. The sky was already dark outside.

"Sorry." He said hastily.

Even though she didn't look up, he forced his words out.

"I didn't mean to leave you by yourself," he drifted off and shook his head, seeing that, still, she refused to look up. "Is it true? You weren't just joking with me? It's true, right?" He demanded, hands trembling a little, "what you told me—is it true?" The second time he asked, his voice shook a little too. Something within the girl quivered at his question.

The candles in the dark room did a little dance in response and the four brown walls seemed to close in on the two of them. He already knew the answer, though. He probably wished he didn't. Pushing back his chair, he stood up, his voice quivered with his next question:

"But would you… have you… gotten rid of it?"

Her head snapped up and her eyes were no longer glazed over at all, but instead, they were glassy and bitter with anger. How dare you, they screamed, how dare you? It seemed that the porcelain doll had heard him after all. Her eyes pierced him through his own and his gut. He did not want to, nor did he need to ask more questions. He already knew the answer. But still, she refused to say anything. Maybe she just couldn't figure out how to answer his question. She held his gaze for a while again before her hands fell into her lap. The room felt cold and clammy despite the warm aroma and coffee wafting around them. She looked back down into her porcelain cup of tea and at its cracked handle. The tea bag was still warm and smelling strong and sweet. They fell back into the silence and the boy, frustrated, upset, and sweaty, sat back down again. The cafe was closing now. She observed the dark sky and the snow that blanketed the grey world beyond the door. Finally, she spoke carefully without any tears, but in a thick voice:

"The cup is cracked. You should just get rid of it."

She stood up and took her brown coat off the back of the chair. As she was fastening the silver buttons slowly, she realized she did not need him to reply. She didn't want a reply. The boy sat still in the cafe, with the small flickering candles dancing slower and slower around him as the room fell into darkness. He could not will himself to stand up because around him, the candles were dimming. The room was turning very dark. She did not look like a porcelain doll anymore. Something inside her stirred and kicked resolutely, spurring her on. The young woman determinedly walked toward the door and toward the grey world outside. She took a deep breath, pushed open the door, and stepped outside. The cafe was closed now behind her. She would never visit it again. The world was grey, and the newly fallen snow was fresh, clean, and sparkling.

KEEPING JERRY

This room's lights were blindingly white. You lay on your back for the first of many visits to come and you're wondering how other women are able to relax with all these white walls while being strangled by the smell of snapping latex gloves and sterile stuff. You hate the ugly gown. It's minty green, but it smells like plastic and rubber.

When you came in earlier, you weren't even sure what you wanted. It was Jerry who urged you to come—for your own good. You felt embarrassed and, for some ridiculous reason, obligated to let the receptionist know that you've never been—it's your first time ever. The receptionist waves you off and told you to take a seat after she handed you the stupid gown. You ask her if it's for now. She rolls her eyes at you and you feel like everyone else in the waiting area is doing the same, so you go and take a seat next to a chubby girl with pink hair and tattoos all over her neck. She glances over at you, smirks amid her gum chewing and goes back to swiping right on Tinder. You're sullen and mad at yourself and you want to jump up and leave. You have to repeat Jerry's name in your head a few times.

Some minutes later, your name is called. The nurse brings you to a room that is only shielded with a curtain, a shade of green darker than the gown. It's the colour of chewed spearmint gum that you can buy from the dollar store. The nurse reminds you that you must strip off all your clothes completely and you wonder if "strip" is really the appropriate word she should be using. You imagine that Pink Girl outside is probably used to the whole stripping thing.

You aren't wearing a bra today because you're wearing Jerry's big blue sweater, so at least there's one less thing to take off. The gown is stupid, it opens up in the front sloppily and the nurse has given you a thin sheet for your lap. You lament taking off Jerry's husky scent.

"Doctor Lee will be with you in a few minutes," she told you. She gestures to the stool that you need to use to get up onto the bed. She instructs you to lay on your back. So you're staring up at the ceiling, hating yourself, hating the nurse, hating Pink Girl, hating latex, and hating everything but Jerry. The curtains are suddenly pushed back, and Doctor Lee enters.

Doctor Lee is actually a man. He looks nice enough, but he's too plump and too happy looking for a doctor. You wonder again why you picked this clinic, with this doctor. It was the closest one to your home. You really just want to get this done with. You already hate Doctor Lee.

He asks you a few questions and then apologizes before helping you place your feet in the stirrups. You wonder if your feet stink and you really hope they don't. You've been wearing socks all day. You tell him, feeling obligated again, that it's your first time going to one of these appointments.

He looks over your form on his clipboard. He asks, do you use tampons? No, you tell him, you can't, you don't know why, it hurts, and you only use pads. Are you sexually active? He asks if you've had sex recently. He's so straightforward with these questions; he's asked them over two hundred times. You think of Jerry. Yes, you tell him, sort of.

With his hand on the inside of your leg, he says you might feel some prodding sensation or pressure down *there*. Nothing to worry about. Easy, easy. No one has ever touched that part of your leg except for Jerry and yourself. You can't see anything, his head is blocked by your pelvis, and you're nervous.

"Relax," Doctor Lee laughs. You hear latex gloves snapping and latching tightly to skin on his wrists.

Your eyebrows furrow as you speculate how the man even got into this line of work. And then you feel it—the familiar and unwelcoming burn as it spread like wildfire up to your abdomen, blooming into the hottest agony from the depths of hell, Inferno, raging right inside your body. Everything is red and the lights are beating, flashing down at you in an SOS panic pattern. You scream and almost kick Doctor Lee in the face. He doesn't flinch and writes some stuff down on to his clipboard. After some minutes, the lights turn back to white and you're back in the ugly mint and white latexy room.

You've calmed down a little bit, so he helps your legs out of the stirrups. He explains that all he's done was press a small cotton tip inside the walls. He didn't even get to the Pap test yet. He removes his gloves and gives you a whole bunch of pamphlets with words that you've never heard of before. The hot pain still settled between your thighs is enough to make you want to die. He's explaining a lot of things, and when you look at his stupid plump and happy face, you realize he probably looks like that because he looks at maybe a good ten vaginas a day, five days a week. There's no cure, he tells you; you don't really know what you expected anyway. You want to punch the doctor. You remind yourself that it was because of Jerry that you came here in the first place. It was your fault, really, because the first time you guys tried to have sex, you were the one who screamed.

Like a baby.

"What the fuck?" he said, sitting up, looking at you with annoyance. He spit on your face as he got off of you. You could tell that he wanted to slap you.

How did you fuck this up again? You were reminded of the white washroom when you were thirteen, trying to shove a goddamn stick of cotton up between your legs. You tried everything—from the one leg on the tub thing to crouching over the toilet. The room turned painfully red each time and you wanted to die. You had to press your blue ice pack against your vagina for hours after every time you tried. Your mom said you probably weren't doing it right; it'll probably take a few tries. You're just scared. You tried every goddamn period until you were seventeen and just gave up. Just resigned yourself to a lifetime of monthly diapers until you hit fifty.

Every time with Jerry, it was like that, but worse. He got pissed off at you. That was why you booked this stupid appointment in the first place.

You leave the room, all dressed, with a bunch of pamphlets in your hand after the doctor tells you to schedule regular appointments. The words "no cure" are ringing in your head. The receptionist gives you a clipboard and form for you to fill out and sign. It's painful to walk. You go back to your seat from earlier—Pink Girl is still there. She pops her gum as you check off some boxes while trying to ignore the pain between your legs. You're really missing your baby blue ice pack right now.

"Sex sucks," she says, without turning to you. You don't have to look to know that she's still swiping right.

You don't turn to look at her either.

"Yeah, it really does," you agree. You finish the form with your signature at the bottom.

But you're back at home later that evening anyway. By nighttime, Jerry is on the mattress with you. It's dark. He asks you how the appointment went; his voice is low, insistent, and you almost feel it caress you with love. Automatically, you tell him everything is okay now; you're pretty much fixed, somehow. The pamphlets were stashed in shreds in the paper shredder bin.

"Good," he says, but he is on top of you already. You're relieved. You bite down hard on your lip so that you don't scream ever again. There is a red monster, breathing fire into you. You are

burning. But with love, you tell yourself, you are burning with love.

JORDAN

I don't know how to run anymore. It's strange—because, you know, I have always been running. It is during the mornings that I once liked to run, out the door by five-thirty, my feet slapping steadily against the paved sidewalk. My muscles used to pull and push in calculated rhythm with my steady movements, propelling me forward as my heart raced with me. But it seemed to change—the sidewalk, I mean. Distorted and unsolid ground that I left in the wake of my running. My chest ached. I'm never fast enough. I was never fast enough. Of course, I can come close, but I was never *her*. But you knew that. You still know that.

We used to do track together. We must have looked so strange, two identical copies of one girl on the track. If we were identical, why did I feel so different? Maybe it was because she wore purple shoelaces and I wore black shoelaces. We would solemnly shake hands at the starting line, but we would both try hard not to smile, her brown eyes usually staring straight through my own. She would squint slightly before turning back to the starting line and back to her position on the track. The gun would crack loudly in the space above and after that, she would burst forward, a runner propelled by spirit and fire. She was so fast that people said she was flying. I didn't know that that race would be her last. It was just the same – the handshake, the squint, the gunshot, then the fifteen hundred metres in her purple shoelaces. The last fifteen hundred metres she would ever run, but only she knew that it would be.

I took the purple shoelaces after that. No one expected me to keep running because I had always been the slower one, the inferior one, a shadow of her sister, concealed under her wings when she took flight—I was shamefully playing it safe. I couldn't even deny this because I knew it was true. There was a part of me that always seemed to resent her. But I love Jordan. The question has always been "Jackie, where's Jordan?" It wouldn't be the fifteen hundred metre event without her. I couldn't tell them. We only have Jacqueline, her sister, the worse sister. No one asked at the next meet. It probably didn't help that I showed up at the next meet in the purple shoelaces, wearing her face, wearing her body. I was her, but the boring, useless version, you know? I was the cold one, the unpopular one, the unfavorable one, the crazy, messed up one, the twin without Cody for a boyfriend. I thought that if I kept running with the purple laces, I could be like her, or even be with her, even if she wasn't there. But it wasn't like that, not even close.

I admit it—I will never be like her. I was and still am always a little slower, a little less than what you wanted her to achieve. I can never be Jordan. I can't even outrun the sidewalk. I would never be able to win.

Even though I write now, I swear that when it happened, I didn't know that she was probably sick too. There was so much she didn't tell us and so much she never even told her own twin sister, the darker half of herself. There was so much my sister took with her, and now, I guess we'll never know.

She died in the way I would have expected someone like her to die. She died very beautifully, majestic and full of sound and fury, in the way she has always been, and in the way that I never could have been. I'm jealous even of the way she died. You found her in the morning with an empty pill bottle on the floor, sprawled across her rumpled bed sheets in her clammy, white skin, her last fifteen hundred event ribbon on her chest. She was beautiful even when she was dead; she was bright and burning right down to her very last breath. I was almost relieved when I saw that she was no longer magnificent after she died. She was like any other dead person.

But I didn't think it was a suicide, did you?

Somebody else must have killed my sister. Wasn't she perfectly fine? Perhaps, you adults thought, her death had something to do with that small moleskine notebook hidden in the back of her closet marked with one number on the first page. However, it was quickly discarded as useless material which none of the adults understood—except me. I was honoured to be the only one that Jordan trusted with her code. To me, it was all very simple. Her code was one number, the number that brought me to the right path to help her. It was all straightforward - she told me what to do, and without questioning, I had given it to her.

A few months too late, I turn to questioning myself while staring straight ahead at the blinking lights in the distance. Did I do it because I truly wanted to help out my sister? Or perhaps I had done it out of spite, because she had everything—and everyone that I wanted. I was jealous, yes. I must have been; I always resented her a little, but I already said that. You loved her—probably more than you loved me. Don't worry, I've known this for a while already anyway. I get it.

Cody's face popped into my mind several times after she died. Honestly! I swear I didn't even know him. Maybe it was the sickness, the voices in my head, urging me to go on, make my own end by myself, like Jordan.

Don't get this wrong, I really loved my sister so much. But did I want her dead? I don't know.

I don't know!

What a weird thing to be unsure about.

Jordan was so beautiful, so brave, so determined, and so loved. I cannot remember her correctly. Maybe my sickness really *has* gotten to me. Two months or so before, she had suggested that we both write out a list.

"Jackie, listen to me," she had said. I didn't know why at the time. Jordan was always a little weird; she had us do random stuff all the time. The list was to contain three numbers of what we wanted most to achieve at some point in our lives. Our numbers two and three were the same: To get married, to travel the world.

I asked her what her number one was. She had left hers blank.

She flashed me her signature mischievous smile, the one expression I could never seem to replicate despite our matching features. "If I told you, you'd have to kill me." She laughed audaciously at my blank expression.

Indignantly, and not to be trumped, I told her, fine, me too. I crumpled up my paper and shoved it down into my pocket.

Then, that one night, I found the notebook on my bed. I found her number one on the list that night.

"Jackie," she had come into my room, "I need to tell you number one on my list. The list. Number one."

I had been quietly working on the reading analysis I had been assigned, the dim desk lamp barely illuminating my messy script scrawled across my lined paper. I didn't speak; I just stopped writing, my pencil poised still above the paper. She sat down on my bed, rumpling the smooth covers that I had carefully laid out that morning.

"I want to fly. Not on a plane, but more like a bird, who can just freely fly wherever, whenever. Imagine all the races I'd win!" She laughed a little, but I could tell it was forced. "I went to the hospital today. I've been going for the past two months."

Really? I hadn't even noticed.

"My leg... I can't feel it sometimes. It hurts. I got scared, Jackie, and you know I never get scared. Running is my life. They said they need to cut it off. I don't want to tell Mom and Dad. I can't. They want me to win so badly and they want me to make it to the Olympics. But I won't be fast or good enough and they won't love me anymore. I don't want to disappoint them." She was silent for a while, and I knew she was crying. But she wasn't. And besides, we all know Jordan doesn't cry.

Then she says it: "I'd rather die than never be able to run again."

Still, I've said nothing.

"Don't tell Cody," she says quietly. I let her sit on my bed in silence for the next five minutes which felt much longer than it should have. Finally, she grabbed my hand and forced me to face her. "Jackie," she said, "you've got to help me fly." She then reached up to touch my face.

And so, the next morning, you found Jordan cold and lifeless, a once blazing fire put out by an empty bottle which once contained my sickness pills on the floor. The bottle had the culprit's name on it. My name. What you didn't find, though, was a crumpled piece of paper that I wrote two months ago, slipped between the last two pages of the notebook.

Jordan never got to number two or three on her list. And I suppose, neither will I, because my number one was different from hers. I expected it to be the same. It pains me to think that maybe we were even more different than I thought. Unlike her, I didn't want to fly. Please don't tell anyone my secret—my number one was to be just like my Jordan, my other half, to be full of sound and fury as she was. Do you get it now? It's your turn to find my number one.

So, in the end, I am standing high up atop the bridge, so high up that I could see all the city lights blinking at me. When I look down, everything, like the shoelaces I wear, is black, so black that I can't even see the water. I can't even see the sidewalk anymore. The wind catches at the second place blue ribbon pinned to the left side of my chest.

"I want to fly with you." I tell Jordan.

Then I jump.

Not yours, Truly

32

FRIDAY THE TWELFTH

Friday the Twelfth

I feel mildly ill. I noticed the boy for the first time today, but I already knew. I knew I didn't like him. I don't know what it was exactly, but he wouldn't have caught my eye on a regular day. He was one of those boys that were ugly, but not ugly enough to pity. He was awkward and lanky, but not outstandingly tall. Just seeing the way he pushed the doors open on his way out frustrated me. The way he moved was a little too sharp; a little too awkward. Why was he like that? Why is the sight of him so appalling? I don't even know his name! I must find out. He aggravates me so. I'll say it again—I don't even know him!

Tuesday the Sixteenth

Today, I see him again. He exits class the same way today, pushing the doors open with those angular arms of his. His elbows jerk forward and his whole body seems to fall forward with the door. It bothers me too much. He sits in the third-last row from the back and in the fourth seat from the right aisle. I still don't know his name! I must find out soon, since the memory of him seems to linger and gnaw away at the back of my mind. At night, when I am about to sleep, I keep thinking about him. I cannot see his face clearly, but I know his hair is a mousy shade of brown. That's it! I've figured it out. My questions are like a mouse in my head, relentlessly gnawing at the back of my mind. I keep seeing him push open the door in the back of the lecture hall—even when I close my eyes I can see it under the darkness of my eyelids. It's like he's taunting me—how infuriating and how rude!

Tuesday the Twenty-Third

I am sitting in the second last row from the back and in the sixth seat from the right aisle today. Although I can only see the back of his head, his mousy brown hair winks at me under the fluorescent lights. Itis hard not to look at it, though. I hate it greatly. I did not even know such hatred was possible. He is hunched down when he scribbles into his notebook and I see that he is left handed. Why, even the way he writes is awkward! His right shoulder leans to the right even though he writes with his left hand. That looks absolutely silly. Now that I sit closer, his sleeves are rolled up as he writes and I can see that he has lightly tanned skin. I am too far to see his face, but I can definitely see the hair. Oh, I wish I could see his face! I feel the mouse gnawing at my brain the entire first hour of the class.

Stop! I try to think the mouse away, but it is unforgiving. I take one of the pills from my pencil case during class and I swallow it with some water. At the end of the second hour, he picks up his books and he leaves through the same door again, taking his mousy brown hair with him. Good riddance, I think!

Friday the Second

Today, I am sitting directly behind him in the third last row and in the fourth seat from the right aisle. To keep that terrible mouse away, I took one of my pills before class. Ha, clever! Not today, mouse, I think to myself. From here, I see that he is actually more muscular than I had earlier assumed. A part of me yearns to feel his tendons and muscles shift under my palms. Today is a warmer day; Autumn doesn't seem to be in a hurry to arrive. He is wearing a plain burgundy shirt and I see muscle ripple through the fabric every time he shifts around. The burgundy clashes with his mousy brown hair. I hate it. Before I know it, the mouse is gnawing at my brain again. I must find out his name soon! Otherwise, the mouse will only continue to eat away at my brain.

Suddenly, I catch it.

The smell. It is coming from him. It is subtle, but I am too clever and I smell it. The mouse chomps at my brain in a frenzy from the stench. Like rotten eggs and sweet maple syrup, the smell is putrid and sweet altogether at once. I take another pill. Oh, how awkward and foreign he looks in his movements as he returns his notebook to his bag. I watch him leave in the same loathsome, awkward fashion through the same door. When I go to my house, I tell Mother with concern:

"Mother, I think there is a mouse in my head."

"Sure there is." She sighs and breathes out a puff of cigarette smoke into Dan's face. Dan leans in with his fat, grey face and mutters something into her ear while looking at me in disgust. I hate Dan and Dan's sweaty hands. I go into my room to tend to the mouse before I can see him kiss her.

Monday the Twelfth

It is terrible. It is so, so, *so* terrible. It seems that the mouse had actually appeared during the night in my sleep! I know this because I woke up this morning with a terrible rash on the back of my left hand. I am certain it is the mouse. How do I know, they may ask? That terrible boy is left-handed, so of course the mouse would gnaw at my left hand to create that terrible rash! It is the most irritating thing. I was even more irritated when I saw Dan still on the living room couch this morning. I got so mad at his fatty hands that I stole his shiny new knife. It was such a clever idea. He *loves* his knives. He spends a good portion of each day organizing them and sharpening them on his whetstone. I will make sure that he will never find this beautiful silver knife.

But here is some more good news! Today, finally, I've managed to sit right next to him. The smell is so strong when I am close. No one else seems to notice it except for me. How are they unable to smell it? It is the most horridly sweet stench. He wears glasses and his face is angular so that the glasses seem too big for his face. My rash feels swollen and I can hear the mouse cackling in my head, so I take a pill from my pencil case. My heart is pounding. I notice he has freckles under his earlobe. The entire two hours, his rotten sweet stench fills my nose—it makes me nauseous. I hate it. I don't hesitate to take another pill as he leaves. He leaves before I find out his name. Next time, I suppose. The mouse is furious.

Tuesday the Twentieth

I took Mother's lotion and some rodent poison from the garage last night. I even bought several mouse traps yesterday afternoon! Before I went to bed, I laid out the traps evenly around my mattress and scattered handfuls of the purple poison tablets in my bedroom. I made sure to put a handful on my nightstand, my carpet, and also in my underwear drawer just to be extra safe. I slept so soundly last night; the mouse is still in my head, but he is resting. I did not even need to take any of my pencil case pills. Unfortunately, my rash still itches. (But it itches more faintly than before, I am sure of it!) I am sitting next to him, as usual. But that's how I did the most devious thing. When he was horribly hunched down and writing, I swiped his eraser and put it into my pencil case. How silly he looked when he couldn't find his eraser! I nearly burst out cackling and I'm sure the mouse did too. Finally, I give it back to him at the end of the class when I ask him his name.

"Thanks for finding my eraser. I'm Cam," he says. His sweaty fingers touch mine for a brief moment and the mouse stirs and begins to gnaw again. Along with the mouse, my something in my chest stirs and aches deeply as our fingers part. I scratch at the patch on my left hand and I take another pill.

Friday the Twenty Third

Cam, Cam, Cam! His name has been ringing gloriously through my head the entire past three days. It makes me rather giddy. The mouse must be giddy too. His voice is strangely soothing for such an irritating person. It just makes him all so much more intriguing. It comes out his mouth like smooth, golden honey. My insides flare with warmth when he speaks. But there is this problem. Every time I hear his voice, the mouse seems to jump—sometimes, he gives me a migraine and inflames my rash as I feel his fat body knock repeatedly against the inside of my skull. I take another two pills. At night, the mouse diligently goes to work and my dreams consist of him opening the door in that awkward motion of his, on repeat. I don't sleep well and I wake up with migraines that the mouse gives me overnight. That sneaky thing! He must be sneaking his way around the poison I have placed around my bed. I must remember to take a pill before I go to sleep at night.

Tuesday the Fourth

I talk to Cam sometimes in class now. I must remember to breathe slowly through my mouth when we speak; it is very difficult to keep my nose from scrunching up. The stench seems to follow me sometimes when I walk back to my house. Sometimes, I follow him as he leaves because there is something about him that frustrates me so. If I can find out what it is, perhaps I can finally silence the mouse.

My brain seems to hum constantly these days despite taking the pills I have been taking. My rash has grown bigger and it itches in every waking hour. How dare he? The mouse must be getting closer.

"Your home is this way too?" Cam asks me in his rich, delicious tone, and I nod and tell him yes. It's not exactly a lie, of course, because the place where I sleep is not my home. When we are walking, he asks me simple questions and we talk some, but it is mostly him who speaks, because it is so soothing for me to hear his voice. I would be enjoying myself if it were not for that putrid stench that makes the mouse go wild. He is so close that it is impossible for me to ignore it. I hate the way he walks. He puts his hands in his pockets awkwardly, as if they have no other place to go. His hands move awkwardly—almost like Dan's! I want to scream at him. Why is he so insufferably annoying? Sometimes he pushes his glasses up his nose, and he does so with his fourth finger very stiffly as if he does not know how to wear them. I grit my teeth every time. When we walk, I must constantly scold the mouse. He keeps nibbling away at the edges of my brain. I really must do something about this nasty rodent. I take another pill after we part ways.

Monday the Tenth

This morning, I put two pills into my water bottle and watch them dissolve. I watch him in class today, just like every day, both enthralled and disgusted at the same time. He never notices when I am watching him because I am very sneaky about it. Do you know how I learned to be so sneaky? I am sneaky because the devious mouse has taught me how. He's not the only one who knows how to be sneaky! This morning, I found blood seeping from the terrible rash. It even smells delicately of his horrible stench. How did the mouse avoid the additional traps I set last night? I even found some cheese and honey to trap him. Mother inquired about it and I told her I was going to catch the mouse. She sniffed, blew a puff of smoke in my direction, and turned back to sit on Dan's lap with his hands around her waist. I hate Dan and his greasy hands. Not as much as I hate the mouse, though. I turn away to take a pill before I return to watching him. Something must be done; how do I get rid of the mouse before he devours my whole brain?

As much as I detest him, I walk with him every day now. He babbles on in his lovely voice while I try to ignore his gracelessness. Of course, it is impossible. Usually, I try to close my eyes or look down. Sometimes, Cam gets excited while telling a story and he grabs my arm or my hand stiffly with enthusiasm. How violent the mouse becomes when he and I come into contact! His hands are always sweaty and warm. I feel nauseous. I must take another pill when I return to my bedroom. Good night. I am turning in early.

Friday the Fourteenth

Let me tell you something—I have absolutely had enough of that damned mouse after last night. I was tossing and turning the entire night, and I could feel my blood boiling despite the chill of the night air. Here is what happened: halfway through that dreadful night, I felt him. The mouse had managed to chew out an opening and I felt him scurrying about through my body! He ran down my arms, across my belly, and up and down my two legs without rest. It was a horrifying sensation. I was scratching and itching at my rash all night. I woke up with the skin on my left hand raw and bleeding—it stings sharply when I wash my hands. Somehow I have scratched at the rash down to the flesh. There was a little bit of pus oozing out, which I soaked up with some toilet paper. I have got to kill this mouse as soon as I can. This morning when I wake up, I take three pills. I shove a handful of the rodent tablets into the pocket of my jacket. Maybe they will subdue the mouse when I am sitting next to him.

Friday the Twenty-First

Last night, I could hear the mouse's breathing. It rasped its hot breath into my body and it whispered strange things in my ears all night.

As I watch him today, he is even more stiff than usual. It makes me want to strangle the gawkiness out of him. He is so fidgety in his seat it makes *me* uncomfortable and his handwriting is even messier than usual; his knuckles are white from gripping his pen. I can imagine his sweaty palms, and my stomach turns at the thought of them touching me. At the end of class, I follow behind him as usual, watching his disjointed movements as he pushes out the door to go home. His motion agitates me so strongly that I just want to pounce on him out of anger. When we are walking, his lovely voice seems strained as he babbles his usual nonsense. Perhaps his voice is starting to become tainted by his awkwardness as well. It would be so, so unbearable if his voice was no longer lovely. At the park, one block before we are to part ways, his babbling stops and he grabs me by the arm, stopping me so that he faces me directly. The mouse is truly restless in his work. He begins to babble again, this time much more nervously. His fingers are sticky against my skin.

I fight it. As the mouth chews faster, I want to throw up. His infuriating babbling makes no sense and I am not listening, but when he suddenly grabs me with warm, greasy hands and presses his awful lips against mine, the mouse pounces about frantically inside, sinking its teeth to pierce what's left of my brain! I can feel my brain innards explode and spill everywhere inside my skull and his teeth sting. They hurt so much! His sickening stench invades my skin and my teeth and my insides churn violently because now I can *taste* the stench. Rotten eggs and maple syrup fill my mouth. How much torture he is causing! Then I devise a great idea right then and there. Thank goodness Winter is arriving, because I am wearing my thicker jacket today, softly lined with fleece on the inside, so that it neatly conceals Dan's silver knife. Smoothly (and not awkwardly at all!), the knife moves to burrow itself into his stomach so that I feel his whole body stiffen completely, all the way up to his mouth on mine. How gracefully the blood pushes its way down the slick wooden handle! I had no idea that something graceful like this could come from inside the boy. The way it moves is not awkward or sharp—nothing like Cam. I am enraptured by its balletic flow down my wrist—so beautiful in its thickness that his sickening stench is drowned in red and I no longer smell it. Inside, up in my head, I feel the mouse panicking as its tail coils around its neck in horror. Finally! Today is the day that I will kill the mouse!

Cam stumbles backward, wide-eyed, mumbling something incoherent before he falls to the ground. I decide to sit next to his twitching body and I wait. I wait patiently for the mouse to die.

I do not know for how long I have been sitting; the sky is dark and the mouse is choking in my head, but it is not enough. He is still alive and desperately chewing away—weaker, but still greedily chewing away. Why is he not dead? The boy is already dead! Or at least I think so—he stopped trembling a while ago. His greasy hands are no longer warm, but I still feel them on my waist. The mouse should be dead! Yet, he continues to struggle stubbornly...

Ugh! He munches down in large bites. The mouse is so resilient! What do I do? What do I do? I know what I have to do. I decide. I am doing it! I pick up the silver knife—still gleaming despite the dark red stains. It is beautiful, it really is. I wonder how much Dan misses it. The man really does not deserve such a beautiful instrument. I doubt he even tried to search for it after I took it. Did I really take it because I wanted to get back at Dan? The silver blade arcs upward toward the mouse—and begins its search for the creature in its hot and pulpous cavern. Warm, beautiful, balletic blood is flowing everywhere. I can't see. Its warmth hugs me everywhere—all over my eyes, my nose, my mouth, and my cheeks.

The knife digs and digs and cuts and cuts. It carves past hair and skin and bone. It hacks away at whatever stands between its blade and him. I do not think it will stop until it reaches the depths in which the mouse has burrowed itself. Ah yes, I feel it! It has taken hold of the mouse by the tail. It writhes in agony as the blade stabs it, yanks it, drags it—it actually drags it out of its cavern! I can't see anything but red melting on red melting on red melting on red— everything is so beautiful. I can't feel anything. I do not even feel his greasy hands. I, too, melt into a hot liquid that slips through anybody's fingers. No one can hold me! I am too sneaky and I am beautiful! So beautiful!

A SMALL THING

"Take good care of yourself, baby."

That's what Ren says when he leaves for work today at exactly 8:06. He always says that. I watch him get into his car. It pulls out of the driveway smoothly. I make sure I press the button for the garage door to shut. Of course I'll take good care of myself, when have I never? The kitchen gets very quiet when he leaves; it is just the same with the rest of the house. It is unsettlingly quiet—I am very used to Ren. A lot of the time when he leaves for work, I find myself wishing for a kitty or maybe even a dog to keep his house alive. Before, when he left for work at the usual time of 8:05 in the mornings, I would sometimes call Alden because he didn't work until the evenings when he taught. He was very nice to talk to when the house got quiet. Sometimes, he would walk down the street with me to The Haven and we could sit and talk over steaming cups of caffeine for hours while Ren was gone.

Right now, his house is so quiet I can hear the ticking of every clock in here. I can hear the kitchen clock ticking just a quarter of a second behind the clock in the piano room. I don't remember how to play the piano since it's been so long since I've been in school, but Ren doesn't like the piano anyway. I don't remember why I pushed to have it in the first place. That was at least two years ago, though.

I begin preparing Ren's lunch because he will probably be coming home soon. Still, my thoughts drift longingly to the warm, grey kitty that might rub itself against my tired legs as I cook and comfort me when my back aches. When I mentioned the kitty to Ren, he was very unhappy and said that we were not ready for, nor did we have the money to afford a feline friend in our house. He told me this as he popped open a third bottle of beer. I did not bring it up any further, but I still think about the kitty a lot. I would have named her Lily, I had decided.

Today is Wednesday, I am making Ren his lunch, I have to remind myself. But my mind wanders back to Lily as I boil the water. She would be soft and wonderful; she would be warm and full of love. I yearn longingly (and nearly in agony!) for her and her tenderness. I think about her small mouth that might open in an adorable little yawn—it is nearly enough to make my heart burst! I wonder what Lily might look like and how she would feel if I held her close to my chest. The water is now bubbling violently and I can feel the steam rising to my face. I open the cupboard. There is not much left; I will have to make a shopping list for Ren to go out grocery shopping. I must remember to tell him tonight. I hope that he will be in a good mood, or else I might not get any groceries other than beer for the rest of this week. I hum the lonely little melody of a piece by

Rachmaninov that I used to play many years ago when I was still in school with Alden. So many years ago. It suppresses some of the silence in the kitchen at the very least. Élégie, I think it's called.

"Oh, Cassie," one of the girlfriends used to say when I was with them, "we all wish ours were more like Ren.

"And yet," she narrowed her eyes very closely to me, "you are unhappy only because he will not bring you home a cat!" All the girlfriends thought this to be very funny and the table would burst into laughter, so I laughed with them, but not really. I am really good at not really laughing. Especially when Ren talks about his co-workers. But I don't really like to go out with the girlfriends—they talk very much about their husbands. All the girlfriends adored Ren.

Ren comes home now. The house is no longer quiet, but it is still very much missing something. I spend too much of my time here—I feel old and full of years even though Ren always says that I am too young to feel that way. I feel achy and empty as he sits down at the table. Standing for a long time makes me tired. I wasn't always like this. At his place I have set his usual glass bottle of beer, his utensils—he preferred his fork on the right side and knife on the left because he was left handed. The spoon was still on the top, though. On the mat was his usual sea green bowl. It wasn't the finest china, but it was his bowl. Only he is allowed to use it. He comes into the kitchen and he gives me a little pat on the head before sitting down at the table. I would love to sink into the comfort of a soft armchair. My body has not been the same since: my back is sore and my breasts ache of heavy fullness. Familiar sounds: the crisp psfff of the metal cap, groaning of the wooden chair, heavy elbows on the table. I think about asking him about the kitty again, but I decide against it. He doesn't seem to be in a good mood today. I am quiet because he is tired from work; he needs his silence, for he has many coworkers to deal with when he leaves again after lunch. I will eat later. I just try to forget about my swollen chest for now.

Clattering of metal utensils on the table make me jump a little bit. My hips are already throbbing.

"Cassie."

Low, slow speaking voice. It is like I am a small child.

"Was there really nothing else you could make, baby? This is not a meal for a grown man."

He likes the peace and quiet; he does not like to be disturbed at lunch. He finishes the rest of his drink and I hear the glass bottom bang the table surface when he puts it down. The chair groans again when he stands up. He comes over, pats me on the head (a little firmer this time) and checks the phone history to see if there have been any outgoing calls today. Satisfied, he asks me if I am still thinking about it. I tell him no, of course not. He smiles at me sweetly, "I need to go back to work now. I love you and I'll miss you."

I go over and pick up the neglected bowl of oatmeal.

"I miss you too, baby," I say to Ren's turned back as he gets into his car. I press the garage door button for him. Watching it shut, I think wistfully of Lily. What a small, wonderful thing she would have been in this house! If only he didn't like his house so quiet. I suppose two small things would be too much for Ren to handle. It wouldn't have been too much for me to handle, though. Oh well, I say to myself, even though I don't feel all too well myself, because my back is still aching. There are other things to deal with first, like Ren's dinner for tonight. Maybe, just maybe, if I can make a good meal, he'll be in a good mood, and everything—and everyone—will be good.

ON YOUR WAY HOME

Some things are unseen—like the thing that is walking behind you. You can't tell exactly what it looks like, but you can hear it. That's how you know it exists. It sounds heavy and it demands your attention. You choose not to give it the attention for which it pleads. It begs. It's whining. You almost give it your attention because it sounds so desperate; it's like it's crying. Something like a kitten's yelp, a couple of seconds before it gets hit by a car running at sixty-two kilometres per hour in a forty zone. Or maybe the sound resembles something more like the owner's cry, a child, who just got slammed violently into their first experience with death? Death's hand is colder than any hand they have ever felt, and harder than any slap from their father felt. It was heavier than anything they had ever lifted and was something so raw that they should not have had to bear witness to at such a young age. Both you and your best friend watched her cat die when you were both in grade six. She cried. You felt cold.

The thing continues to plod behind you, nagging. Its footsteps ring throughout the dark space. You should probably do something about it. You've been ignoring it for a while now. It seeks your attention desperately, thirsting for it. It's hungry, too; you can feel it. It's not quite touching you, but it's hovering inches away from the skin on your shoulder. Groans creak from the bottom of its throat and you have to try not to jump. It's so much closer to you than you thought. Maybe it's just doing this because there is nothing else in this barren landscape. You do your best to pretend everything is normal.

Don't look, you tell yourself, it's best to ignore it.

It's grey where you are and there is not much light anywhere. The only light you have is this little flashlight you have on your lanyard, next to all your keys and the tacky blue keychain your best friend gave you from her trip to Asia. If you press the red button twice, it will turn on. But what will any light from your feeble keychain flashlight do? It's too dark for it to serve any purpose. Your thumb hovers over the button, for a millisecond maybe—were you considering pressing it? No, of course not. You don't want to be involved with this thing. You just want to get home.

You figure that if you try to fight this thing, you'll probably lose. You can tell it's a big creature from the way you hear it moves, the way it functions, and the way it breathes. Its breath is hot and cold at the same time and it smells rotten and sour. It reminds you of those rare times when you accidentally turned the water too hot in the shower. Your skin was suddenly burning so much that it felt cold in a fiery way. That's how its breath felt on your back. It's so loud that you shudder at the very thought of even looking into its face. You wonder if you say its name—will it grow bigger? Will it fight back at you? Will it gain strength because somebody finally admitted its existence? You don't really want to test it out. You stride along and try to block out its sounds. It whines behind your back again. Your eyes try to dart away from the shadow that stalks you along the pavement.

It's hard to ignore it because of the prominent way it moves along behind you as you walk. It drags itself along not only by its feet, but with numerous hairy tentacle-like things that you can also hear scraping along the ground. You imagine its tentacles wrapping around all your limbs—a tentacle per limb, one around your torso, one around your neck, and one pressed against your mouth. Spiked fur that could pierce into your neck and inject venom into your blood. It could easily choke you even if it chose not to pierce you.

"Fuck off, leave me alone," you mutter uneasily. It doesn't, of course. It's persistent—unsurprising. You didn't want to face this thing, but you're starting to get too scared to ignore it any longer. You thought you could have ignored it all the way home. Can you do it? Can you even face this huge thing?

You're about to turn around, but you stop yourself. Not a good idea, probably, you tell yourself. You wonder if this thing will follow you all the way home. You don't want to deal with this thing in your own home. You want to go to bed and get a good night's sleep. Your best friend has been suffering from insomnia lately and she it sounds pretty bad. You're just glad you're not the one who has it and you can still fall asleep. Probably not if this thing follows you home though, you realize.

You feel it. You feel how dark it is. It's sticky and sandpapery at the same time. Its skin hurts to the touch. Is it possible to defeat the thing without touching it? You imagine that the skin of your hand will blister and bubble upon encountering the thing's skin, eventually disintegrating down to bone in less than a few seconds. You shove both your hands, in fists, deep into your pockets.

What if the thing follows you home, decides not to kill you, and lives there instead? It would probably damage all your furniture and knock over everything. Set fire to the walls, even. Melt the toilet with one touch. There is no way you can let this thing into your house. There is one more block until you reach home. One more block to deal with the thing behind you.

Half a block.

In a few more steps, it will be a third of the block. It's now or never.

You take a deep breath and whirl around, ready to fight the ugly, tentacled, and hairy thing and tell it to fuck off.

Instead, you find yourself facing your best friend. This is where she takes a right to go to her street and goes home as usual. You can't believe you were about to tell her to fuck off.

"Good night," she says to you, donning her sweet smile that you've seen a billion times. You watch her as she takes a step back. She had the same sweet smile after she finished crying in grade six. She looked pleasant—serene even. You love her so much.

Good night, you say back to her, and give her a hug. You feel cold all over. It's not because of the creature. You didn't even touch it. You watch your best friend leave. The thing is no longer unseen. You can see it and it's eating her face. It's all over her face; the tentacles are everywhere and acid is dripping from its hair. It goes home with her.

DEAR LITTLE LOVE

Dear Little Love,

I think things at home should probably be settled down by now. How are you doing? How is Dee doing? I hope that the both of you are doing well. It has been a while, hasn't it? I can imagine you now, surprised that you've received a letter. It should have been at least two years now. You're probably taller and more slender, beautiful as ever, and the portrait of a defiant young woman who always marches forward without hesitation. I hope you aren't still worrying about your freckles on your cheeks. I've always told you how much I love them. I hope that by now you have learned with time to love them too. Now that you are a woman, you may find that there are so many things in your life that want to whisk you off your feet much too quickly. Maybe it is the prospect of having potential suitors, new working opportunities, or even the fact that Dee is growing up too. I bet she's growing up to be beautiful too, just like her sister.

But, my little love, let me tell you a secret. You must take a deep breath and walk slowly. Many things around you will want to rush you and hurry you, so that your feet will find themselves off balance. If you feel like you need more time, that is perfectly fine. Time is something you can surely find within the night. There is something about the night which makes it last forever. If you stay up well past sundown, there is something that suspends itself, invisible, but quite positively there, buried deep within the dark cloak of the night. And if your heavy eyelids do not drop, then the night is forever yours as long as you don't check for the time. There is no rush. The night is there until you do decide to finally let your eyelids close—this is what I did for many nights when I did not know how to speak to you, your father, and worst of all, Dee. Dee was so little; how could I tell her? I worry so much. I worry that I do not have enough time. So this is how I try to buy my time before I leave.

You used to throw the biggest tantrums before Dee came along. Remember to be patient with both her and your father. I know Dee can be annoying sometimes, but aren't all little girls at some point? I remember how loud and hot-headed you would be when I refused to buy you a cake every time you came with me to the market! So what I am telling you is to be understanding, for I know how much you love her. Keep in mind—both you and I were annoying little girls at one point too! I remember that I was quite terrible as a child too. As a little girl, I used to scream whenever your Uncle Jeb got a treat and I didn't. So you see, you must try to understand Dee.

I, too, struggle with forgiveness sometimes. But I've managed to forgive your father. I haven't told you girls yet, but when I finally admitted to him that I would be leaving, he was livid that I had hidden this from him for months. He didn't speak to me for a week and he slept with his back turned against me in our bed. He didn't even touch me.

I tried to speak and he tried to listen, but he was still hurt. He's stubborn and easily flustered, but your father works very hard—you must be patient with him. He has trouble showing it sometimes, but he loves you two very much. He is only harsh to you because he cares and loves you. I understand that he loves me too, just as I love him. He is a good man. Although he may be much older than you and Dee, he is, still, only human. Just as I am for you and Dee, I am afraid for him as well—that he might forget that he, too, is still loved. When I am gone, he will need reminders that he is still loved. If only I could have physically poured out my love into a bowl for the three of you before I left so that I could be comforted in knowing that the three of you will always have a reminder that you are loved.

I was so tormented I cried out to God every night in the darkness. I told Him that there were many things left to do, I told him: "there are many things that I still want to do for them!" I'm sure God heard me, but, still, I was consumed with anguish as soon as I realized that there was this darkness inside my body that would never leave me. It was then that I realized how weak I was. But as it killed me softly and slowly with every day, God gave me comfort in the moon. Watch the moon through your window, if you can, on the nights you stay up, looking for time. Sometimes the clouds cover her so that the night turns thick and murky so that it is faint, and other times it cuts cleanly and clearly through the darkness like a sharp knife. But, you see, it is always there. Never forget about the moon. Think about all the years she has been undeviatingly shining, before you were born, I was born, and even well after everyone you know has gone from this earth. Sometimes the darkness may seem thick, know that, even then, God has carefully hung her there up high in the sky, and she will not fall. Steadily, like my love, she will always be there, and unlike me, she will never leave you. As Dee grows older, you must remind her that you love her. When you have your own children, you must remember to remind them how much they are loved, just as their mother was and is and always will be. Remind them, Little Love, that there is always someone there, loving them. If they are struggling to remember, tell them to draw a breath, wait for the night, and take a look at the moon in the same way I have told you to look too. Oh, how I wish I could see you get married someday! But that is selfish of me to think of now. My heart is so full as I write this, I feel as though it may burst.

Things will get busy, but take your time. Never hate yourself for whatever happens during the day. Don't carry your hot anger over into the next day. The cooling night will always be there at the end of the burning day. The moon is shining brightly as I am writing to you. Tonight, it is clear, steady, and it slices through my window to light up my entire bedroom. It almost feels like tonight will last forever. Again, I am being too selfish. I am just looking for time. I hope that it will shine the same way when you are reading this. Don't forget to look up and admire her whenever you find yourself enveloped in the comfort of the cool night because maybe, just maybe, I may be watching her too.

Good night, my little love. I hope to see you one day again!

Love,

62

THE GIRL

The girl, an overview

Bea was one of those gifted kids that tested into that stupid program where you needed to go to a special school a distance away from the normal local ones. She hated how she had to bus all the way to some other school downtown and south of the suburbs, when she could have walked ten minutes instead to Redland Secondary. As far as she knew, she was very mediocre. Average, if you were being nice. If there was a competition for being most mediocre, she would probably win. Yeah, sure, maybe she was a little sharper than her classmates when it came to math, but that was it. That was only because she fell in love with geometric shapes back in senior kindergarten. She was good with shapes. As she was growing up, Bea encountered many shapes. When she was in kindergarten, she learned the simple ones: squares, triangles, and circles. In middle school, three-dimensional shapes were introduced. Bea took to those ones easily—triangular prisms, cylinders, and cubes. In high school, she discovered new and complex shapes that she found much harder to grasp— billowing hourglasses, matching C cups, and perky, tight, heart-shaped bottoms. Despite her accumulated knowledge of various shapes, at the age of twenty-two and a half, Bea felt like she had pedalled backwards, because the only shapes she knew and still found understandable were simple squares. She obsessed over them so much that she preferred a lot of her things in perfect squares— even her food.

"Who even eats square cookies?" her roommate would often tease and laugh. Bea was inexplicably attached to squares. She even went out to buy square plates. She threw out all her old, round-shaped plates—they didn't match her aesthetic, she told her roommate.

Bea had always liked the way her mother had made her cakes, though, even though they weren't square. They were nice, round, fluffy, and never too sweet. She used to bake them for Bea every Friday. That's why Fridays had always been her favourite day—not because it was the start of the weekend, but because she would have always been rewarded with that familiar aroma of vanilla and honey when she came home at the end of the day. Come to think about it, Bea had only become obsessed with squares not too long ago.

Everyone used to say that Bea's mom was the best baker in the area. When she started to skip some of her weekly baking sessions, Bea took over and began to bake on Fridays. Everyone said Bea's cakes were just as good as her mother's; her special touch must run in the family.

Bea didn't get it. Special touch? No such thing.

Baking wasn't that hard, Bea realized. A cake really only consisted of flour, sugar, butter, eggs…and some milk here and there…

Bea's hands hover with uncertainty above the large bowl. She's watched her mother bake cakes countless times for more than two decades, but she's never been able to replicate her cakes. Every cake Bea ever attempted to bake seemed to pale in comparison—whether in flavour, texture, or appearance. She even tried to make them square instead of round. And then round instead of square. The cakes were still terrible and that was why she started to bake cookies instead. They were easier, anyway. Cookie cutters worked so cleanly—it was so satisfying to see the sharp edges cut precise shapes into the soft dough. They were reliable and consistent, always cutting the same perfect shape, and it always made Bea feel better.

Bea, in the middle of swishing the whisk around the bowl, asks herself if she's making cookies or attempting a cake. She's forgotten, *again*, so she goes over to the sink and dumps the lumpy contents into the drain. The sink makes a groaning sound before the kitchen settles back into its stillness accompanied by the low hum of the fridge. Bea's phone, upon receiving a message, goes off against the kitchen table across the room. Her roommate will be coming back soon.

Upstairs, to shower and change, Bea reminds herself; into the sweatshirt with long sleeves, she tells herself, as she is clearly incapable of remembering things. On her way out of the kitchen, she passes by the table once more and her eyes accidentally fall on the silver shapes lying on the checkered spread.

Cookie cutters. Of course she was making cookies; she hasn't made a cake for years. What the hell? She'd given up on that a long time ago. How could she forget? Just like her mother used to forget that Friday was Cake Day. She takes the medium-sized square cutter with her back to her room.

Her shower stung, like usual. What else is new? She hated showers. She knew that, in a couple of days, the stinging showers would turn into stinging and itchy showers, and then just itchy showers. She dries herself off quickly afterward.

After Bea has managed to put on her sweatshirt—one arm through each sleeve at a time—she allows herself to fall back, heavily, on to her mattress. She wants to feel better because she's wearing her favourite sweatshirt—the dark-red one with sleeves that cinch at the wrists so that they don't fall up her arms whenever she reaches upward. She wonders if someone could still have a special touch even when they've forgotten everything else—like how to bake a cake, or even that Friday was cake day.

Bea had promised herself that she would never turn out to be like her mother; her roommate also always assured her that she wouldn't turn out to be like her mother. "Because science said so," she would explain with a lot of big words. Bea even took the tests, didn't she? Negative, each one confirmed. But why did she keep going back to the clinic every month or so, asking if she could be tested again? Maybe because the results could have been wrong, the voice in Bea's head said; after all, the test was conducted by humans. Humans are always erroneous in one way or another. At least Bea knew that *she* was erroneous. There's no way someone could be so ridiculously obsessed with squares without having something wrong with them.

From downstairs, she hears the door of her and Angela's small townhouse swing open and the sound of someone shuffling to take off their shoes. She knows she will have to face her roommate soon. She stands up and holds the silver square in front of her face. She inhales, and exhales. Bea decides, again, that there will be no circles for her today. Not today, or ever, probably. The square goes into her pocket.

The girl's roommate

Bea's roommate was called Angela. Angela moved into Bea's cozy townhouse in her second year of college because she's known Bea since high school. Besides, Bea's place is closer to her school anyway. Angela is doing her major in psychology and in astrophysics. She tries to put her studies to good use outside of the classroom. She tries to talk to her friends; she tries to make them feel better by easing their mind, or so she thinks. On many Fridays in high school, Angela got to try some of Bea's mom's cakes. She had to admit, the cakes were really something. Fluffy, melt-in-your-mouth sort of stuff. She makes fun of Bea's square cookies that she always seems so fond of baking in lieu of cakes on Friday—AKA cake day—because she feels like Bea always needs to lighten up a little bit more. Bea worries too much, she finds. Angela likes to make a lot of bad jokes and tells them to Bea. She tries to push Bea out of her shell, to get her to "go out!", live, and be happy. She *knows* that Bea would feel a lot better if she just spent more time outside with friends. She *knows* how people from town talk about Bea's mom—the things they say about her outside of her exceptional baking. Angela tells people that she *knows* Bea. She's been living with her for several years now; she can testify that Bea is definitely not crazy and Bea is not her mom.

Angela's voice rings out through the house—high pitched. Every single day, she came home, calling out to Bea as soon as she put her foot through the door. Today is Friday. She feels a little disappointed when she doesn't smell the sweet and warm aroma of chocolate, flour, and heaven when she opens the door to her and Bea's place. It wasn't that she was craving cookies or anything—she was just disappointed in herself more than anything. She supposed she'd have to try and give a talk to Bea again.

The girl's mom

Bea's mom was great. One of those cool moms, you know—or, at least, before she started going crazy. She was a journalist for the local Tribune, but everyone said she should have started her own bake shop instead, because of all the amazing stuff she baked. A shop probably would have done well, because everyone in the neighbourhood was always asking her to bake them one of her cakes for special occasions—birthdays, baby showers, sometimes even weddings. Not once did her cakes disappoint.

After Bea hit tenth grade, her mom stopped baking on some Fridays. After Bea hit twelfth grade, her mom had stopped baking completely. She didn't bake during the week, nor did she bake on the weekends. She quit her journalist job soon after that. She started going to the clinic pretty often. Bea went with her there, and it was there that she found out the chances were fifty-fifty for herself. Soon after that, the whole neighbourhood discovered all of this was because Bea's mom had apparently gone crazy. She became so crazy that she ended up forgetting she had a daughter who she herself had nicknamed Bea. A little later, she couldn't even recognize Bea. The whole neighbourhood claimed she was crazy because whenever she went outside her house, they would see her walking on the lawn in endless circles. She even talked in circles. She probably thought in circles too. That's what crazy women do, they pointed out—Bea's mom was loopy. She would walk around their front lawn, drooling a bit as she spoke in a slurred, unarticulated fashion as people watched either walking by or from safety behind their windows. She walked and spoke almost like a drunk, except she wasn't drunk. Sometimes, she spoke to herself, and other times she spoke to something that wasn't there. She had this weird way of moving— twitches where her arms would tense and involuntarily jerk on their own. She hit her head soon after that, because she couldn't walk straight. She lost her balance and fell down frequently, and that time, she fell for the last time. Walking down the stairs ended up being a hazard for a crazy woman like her.

Too bad, poor girl, what a shame, no more cakes. At least she left Bea with her special touch, some people said. Bea went and took the test at the clinic right after she died.

The girl, but more

Today is Friday. Maybe she should have just gone "fuck it," and thrown the mixture she was making into the oven anyway instead of just dumping it down the drain. Bea wondered if it would be possible to reach her hand into the drain and somehow scoop up the contents she had thrown out an hour ago. She has second thoughts, because she realizes how this would probably be stupid and impractical; she almost gags because she imagines touching the mold and gunk in the pipes. Why did she even consider that in the first place? She really needs to keep herself in check. How long has it been since her last test? The clinic staff recognize her now. It was probably because they felt bad for her, because even though the test results kept showing up as negative, they always let her come back. They offer pity smiles when she walks in. She wonders how many more times they will allow her to retake the test.

But Bea's convinced that she's crazy, no matter how many times the results come back as negative. Only a crazy person would eat only square cookies. She's certain she's crazy, as much as she desperately wants not to be. How long would it be before the neighbourhood started looking at her the same way they looked at her mom?

She had heard Angela come in, but she doesn't really feel like talking because she doesn't feel like another counselling session today. Her fingers find their way to the comfort of the square that she's shoved in her pocket. It's cool, clean, and familiar.

The girl's fingers

Bea's fingers were long and slender. They matched Bea's mom's fingers. They were always rough around the knuckles, because she hated the sticky feeling of moisturizer. A little dry, because she used them to knead cookie dough every Friday and she only used hot water to wash them. Bea's fingers liked to trace shapes. Ever since she had fallen in love with two-dimensional shapes at five years old, she often found herself tracing squares on any piece of paper she could find. It was a habit. Bea loved squares. She loved how they were so balanced, symmetrical, and altogether a stable and reliable shape. None of that scalene triangle bullshit where none of the angle degree numbers matched. Her obsession bloomed after Bea's mom left. She traced them against the skin on her wrists, her forearms, her thighs, her calves, and at night, when she was laying down, her stomach and her chest. Bea's fingers were very important because they grounded her, yanked her back into reality, and brought her back to sanity. After her last visit to the clinic, Bea's fingers scrambled through her sock and underwear drawer to weed out her polka-dotted ankle socks and polka-dotted panties. Her fingers were swift and worked fast. These were the two things that Bea knew, for sure, kept her intact—her fingers and squares. But even when her fingers tried to trace squares, they were never perfect. She felt it on her skin. The squares were ugly and unproportionate. They were characterized by uneven, unequal edges and non-right angles teetering at ninety-seven degrees or eighty-two degrees. She wondered if her mother ever tried to ground herself in the same way she did. Would it have worked? If it did, maybe she wouldn't have turned out so crazy in the end.

She found that only perfect squares could cut cleanly and with gratifying precision. Bea was angry at her fingers because no matter how hard they tried, they could never draw four clean one-and-a-half-inch lines at perfect ninety degree angles. So, to placate their angry master, Bea's fingers liked to hold the square cookie cutter more often than not. Even when she wasn't baking cookies. They held onto the cookie cutter even when she was taking the bus or in class. These were crazy fingers on a crazy girl.

The girl, in squares

Bea had a tendency to drown herself in squares whenever things outside of her body suffocating her. She drew them all over, any time. She even traced small ones on the side of her thigh when Angela was smothering her with her big words and huge scholarly terms. She even drew them when she noticed small things, like Angela's silver hoop earrings. Someone breathing in deeply, then blowing out the air through pursed, rounded lips. Highlighters screeching across lined paper. Mouths slurping noodles. Bright LED ceiling lights. All these things suffocated Bea, made her gag.

She threw out her old tablecloth—the one with decorative spirals—and bought new black-and-white checkered ones from Walmart.

Bea was a very careful person. She was careful to keep her

appearance clean-cut and precise, straight and sharp, balanced and sane. That is why she tried to make absolutely sure that Angela wouldn't find out about her square addiction—to Angela, how stupid and absurd would that be?

"Hey, today was *super* tiring," Angela says when she comes in and sees Bea walking down the stairs. She's bubbly, as usual. "How are you feeling? Any regularly shaped circular cookies for normal people today? Or any cookies at all?" she tries to joke as she tosses her jacket and keys on the sofa.

Bea smiles, on the outside. "No. No circles for me. I didn't feel like making any cookies today, sorry," she apologizes, and adds hastily, "Square or not."

Angela smiles back in response.

The square is still in the left pocket of her sweatpants. Bea feels its cool familiarity through the material and against her leg. Her fingers reach down, touch the chilled metal, ground their owner. The coolness yanks her back into her body and pins her to the ground. She asks herself: how is someone even addicted to squares? She hates herself for it. Not Angela, nor anyone else would ever understand why Bea was so attached to her squares. Maybe it was because a lot of people didn't really ever try to bake. Or it may have been because Bea always wore long sleeves. Or maybe it was because they never actually *knew* Bea's mom. Or maybe it was because they never had showers that stung and itched at the same time. As a result, Bea would probably never let anyone see or understand how satisfyingly the silver, stainless-steel square's right angles and perfect edges fit, aligned, parallel to Bea's wrist line, perpendicular to her long fingers, and sank into skin like dough. The world might laugh naïvely, just as Angela would always tease—who even likes to eat square cookies?

Not Bea, that's for sure. That's what she realized. She didn't even like squares all that much. She just couldn't bring herself to eat round cookies like everyone else, that was all.

ABOUT THE AUTHOR

Giselle Chan is the author of Not yours, Truly. She has written a lot of stories that clutter up her Google Drive, so she put them all together in a book to free up some space. She is a young writer based in Toronto, Canada, as well as an accomplished badminton athlete and pianist. Although often claiming to be busy, she can usually be found napping or watching The Office. She is currently working on her second book.